Dear Parents:

Children learn to read in stages, and all children develop reading at different ages. **Ready Readers™** were created to promote children's interest in reading and to increase their reading skills. **Ready Readers™** are written on two levels to accommodate children ranging in age from three through eight. These stages are meant to be used only as a guide.

### Stage 1: Preschool-Grade 1
Stage 1 books are written in very short, simple sentences with large type. They are perfect for children who are getting ready to read or are just becoming familiar with reading on their own.

### Stage 2: Grades 1-3
Stage 2 books have longer sentences and are a bit more complex. They are suitable for children who are able to read but still may need help.

All the **Ready Readers™** tell varied, easy-to-follow stories and are colorfully illustrated. Reading will be fun, and soon your child will not only be ready, but eager to read.

# If I Had A Hippo

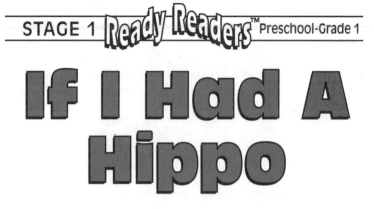

Written and Illustrated by J. Ellen Dolce

Big Book of ANIMALS

Modern Publishing
A Division of Unisystems, Inc.
New York, New York 10022

If I had a hippo, I'd name it Pippo.

If I had a poodle,
I'd name it Noodle.

If I had a shark,
I'd name it Clark.

If I had a whale,
I'd name it McHale.

If I had a boa, I'd name it Noah.

If I had a bunny,
I'd name it Sunny.

If I had a sheep,
I'd name it Bo-Peep.

If I had a dragon,
I'd name it Flagon.

If I had a parrot,
I'd name it Garrot.

If I had a lizard,
I'd name it Wizard.

If I had a clam, I'd name it Sam.

If I had a squid,
I'd name it Sid.

If I had a pony,
I'd name it Baloney.

Well, I don't have
a hippo
or a poodle
or a shark
or a whale
or a boa
or a bunny
or a sheep
or a dragon
or a parrot
or a lizard
or a clam
or a squid
or a pony...

But I have a turtle,
and I named him...
Fred!